TASK FORCE DELTA
FIRST STRIKE

Craig Simpson

First published in 2012
by Franklin Watts

Text © Craig Simpson 2012
Illustrations by David Cousens © Franklin Watts 2012
Cover design by Peter Scoulding

Franklin Watts
338 Euston Road
London NW1 3BH

Franklin Watts Australia
Level 17/207 Kent Street
Sydney, NSW 2000

A CIP catalogue record for this book
is available from the British Library.

ISBN: 978 1 4451 0696 0

1 3 5 7 9 10 8 6 4 2

Printed in Great Britain

Franklin Watts is a division of Hachette Children's Books,
an Hachette UK company.
www.hachette.co.uk

The Real Delta Force

Task Force Delta is inspired by one
of the United States' top-level secret
military units, the 1st Special Forces
Operational Detachment — Delta (1SFOD-D)

also known as

Delta Force

Delta Force's main missions are direct, counter-terrorism
action. They also carry out many secret assignments
including hostage rescues and raids behind enemy lines.

Delta Force (also called "The Unit")
is based at Fort Bragg, Carolina, USA.

Delta Force's motto is:
"Surprise, Speed, Success"

Major Nathan Connor
Highly decorated
Commander of Delta Force.
Transferred from the 75th
Ranger Regiment. Speaks
five languages including
Pashto.

Lieutenant Danny Crow
Second in command.
Came top of his class in Special Forces'
"Operative Training Course".

Lieutenant Jacko Alvarez
A former Navy Seal and
weapons expert.

Sergeant Major Sparks
Comms and intel expert and
veteran of several Special
Forces units before being hand-
picked for Delta Force.

**Master Sergeant
Ben Saunders**
Transferred from 75th
Ranger Regiment. An
expert in survival skills
and demolition.

**Sergeant First Class
Sam Wilson**
World-class sniper skills led to
recruitment into Delta Force,
despite being just 19 (usual
minimum age 21).

CONTENTS

CHAPTER ONE
First strike

Kabul, Afghanistan

Tariq's big day had arrived. He'd never felt so nervous. Outside Kabul's *Pul-e-Khishti* mosque, he paused to wrap a blanket around his shoulders against the bitter wind. He hurried to the bus depot, taking a short cut past the bustling stalls and colourful booths of the ancient *Ka Faroshi* bird market. In his rush along the narrow street, he bumped into several large domed wicker cages. The fighting *kowks* perched inside flapped their wings and squawked at him. Angry stall owners threw up their arms and cursed as he vanished into the crowd.

At the bus depot, Tariq boarded his battered old school bus. He slid onto the driver's seat, reached forward and started the engine. He gripped the steering wheel tightly to stop his hands from shaking.

Out in the city's tightly packed traffic, Tariq edged the bus forward towards the Afghan National Army checkpoint ahead. Checkpoints did not worry him, though. He saw them every day, and the soldiers and policemen waved him through. To them he was just a friendly school-bus driver.

Mushi waited at the bus stop with his hands shoved deep in his pockets, kicking stones into the gutter. He was still half asleep and he couldn't stop yawning. School was such a pain, he thought. There was a kite fighting festival the following weekend and his kite still needed its finishing touches; an extra coating of ground glass on the strings so, when he battled with other competitors, his string would cut theirs and he'd win. The bus pulled up and Mushi clambered aboard. As usual, his friend Kemal had saved a seat for him in the third row.

Tariq crunched the gearbox and pulled off. It was almost time. The bus was full now, crammed with boys dressed in their smart school uniforms.

Tariq despised them and their privileged backgrounds. Their fathers could afford to pay the school fees. Tariq knew a few had grown rich through work paid for by the American infidel, and that fact alone was enough for him to hate them. Tariq shut out all the jabbering young voices and focused hard on the road ahead. The traffic was flowing freely now.

Tariq reached a junction and turned left, heading for the city centre. Startled, Mushi blinked and shot bolt upright. He knew something was wrong. He called out to the driver, "Why are we going the wrong way?"

Tariq had prepared for this. "There are road closures. We must go this way," he lied. His heart pounded in his chest, but he tried to remain calm. Voices inside the bus trailed off and Tariq sensed the growing unease behind him.

"No there aren't. I want to get off!"

Tariq ignored Mushi. Instead, he pressed the accelerator pedal and increased speed.

"Stop!" other boys were calling out.
Tariq began to pray, his lips moving silently...
"*Allahu Akbar...*" He pulled out to overtake a car slowing down for an army checkpoint.

Mushi watched in horror as the bus roared on, busting through the plastic barriers and scattering the armed men in uniform. He turned to look back. The soldiers should have tried to stop the bus. They should have raised their guns. Now it was too late.

Tariq saw the coffee house at the end of the street. It was no secret that many local Afghan interpreters employed by the Americans visited it. To him, these men were traitors, worse than dogs.

"Where are we going? Let us off!" Mushi demanded.

Without warning, a donkey and cart piled high with vegetables trotted from a side street. Tariq saw them but kept on course. The bus rocked as it struck the donkey and the boys screamed. In desperation, Mushi leapt forward, grabbed hold of Tariq and wrestled with him, trying to make him stop.

Tariq was too strong. He pushed the accelator pedal to the floor and the engine groaned. Buildings flashed by in a blur. Mushi tried punching Tariq, and then yanked his beard. He tore out a handful of hair, but fell backwards onto the floor.

Tariq didn't flinch. He reached for a switch on the dashboard. Behind the panel wires coiled under the bus to a bomb fixed on the fuel tank.

With his other hand he yanked the steering wheel and the bus veered sharply right. The bus mounted the pavement.

Tariq had been promised Paradise. No longer would he a humble bus driver. He was to be *fedayeen* — a martyr. His was the first strike.

Mushi screamed as the bus ploughed into the front of the coffee shop. Tariq pressed the switch.

A tall plume of black smoke rose over the city.

CHAPTER TWO
Spring offensive

Camp Delta

Connor had been eating some spicy chicken wings when the text came through. It had ordered him to report to the Ops Room immediately.

Grim faces greeted Connor and his men when they got there five minutes later. General Patterson, head of CENTCOM — Central Command — wasted no time in introducing them to Colonel Rogers, Chief of Combined Black Ops, and his team of intelligence officers.

"You've seen the news feeds," Rogers began.

Connor nodded. "Yes, the bus bomb in Kabul."

"You can imagine what the media back home are saying. The Taliban have begun their spring offensive early this year and caught us on the hop. It's just the beginning, too. We have good reason to believe they're planning a major campaign of attacks, abductions, assassinations and suicide bombings. Gentlemen, a decision's been made at the highest level. Innocent lives are at stake. We're going on the offensive."

Connor fidgeted uneasily in his chair as Colonel Rogers hooked up his laptop, projecting the files onto a large screen. The first was a detailed map. "OK, this is what we know," Rogers continued. "Intel is sparse. Bad weather has restricted our use of drones, and the Taliban have been wise enough to limit their phone use and radio transmissions. However, interrogations of recently captured insurgents near to Doshi and Jabal Saraj have yielded a few pieces of the jigsaw. We believe armed insurgents are on the move and gathering in small groups in the Hindu Kush mountains. The leaders are going to meet with this man..." Rogers paused while he switched files. "Mullah Khan. This guy's as bad as they come. He's the one pulling the strings. Deal with him and the insurgents will be leaderless and in disarray."

Connor leaned forward and studied the photo of a tall, bearded man. He had scarring down the left side of his face. "Do we know where and when the meet will take place, sir?"

"No. If we did there'd be no need for me to talk to you, major. Instead, I'd be arranging an air strike." Rogers returned to the map of the Hindu Kush mountains and pointed vaguely. "Most likely, they'll get together somewhere around here. There are lots of old silver mines. Perfect for hiding out."

"So, just let me get this straight, sir," Connor interrupted. "You want Delta Force to locate Mullah Khan and find out when and where the meeting will take place, so you can then arrange a targeted air strike."

Colonel Rogers nodded. "Got it in one, major. Radio us the co-ordinates and let our F-16s do the rest. Naturally, if the opportunity arises, feel free to take out Khan yourselves."

It sounded so simple, but Connor knew nothing could be further from the truth. "I foresee one or two problems, sir."

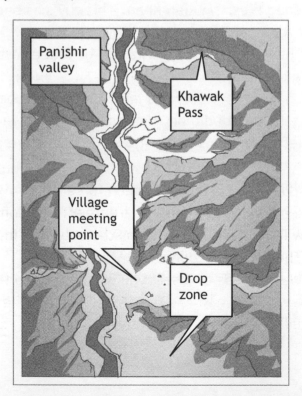

"Thought you might, major. Fire away."

"Firstly, how do we get even close to them?
Blocked by snow, most of the mountain roads
are still impassable by vehicle, and it would take
days on foot. Also, the only ground entry point
is via the Panjshir valley. And that means going
through the gorge at Dalan Sang. We'd be spotted
and picked off like sitting ducks, just like the
Russians were back in the 1980s. Alternatively,
if we helicopter in they're bound to hear us
coming, especially as the region is supposed to
be crawling with Taliban."

"There is a way, major."

Danny groaned. "I think Colonel Rogers has a
HALO jump in mind, sir. It's the only way in."

Connor shuddered. HALO, or high-altitude-
low-opening, parachute jumps were extremely
hazardous at the best of times. The lengthy free-
fall phase could carry you way off target, and if
you left it a second too late to open your chute
you'd hit the ground with such force that two
broken legs were almost guaranteed. But Connor
knew Danny was right. It was the only way in.

"Then what?" Connor countered.

"We're going to insert you on the trail to the
Khawak Pass, major," Rogers explained. "There's
a small village that's been largely deserted for

the last fifteen years. There, you'll rendezvous with our local contact. His name is Hamid. He should be able to assist you." The colonel introduced one of his team. "This is Lieutenant Bradley. He's an ex-navy SEAL and is Hamid's liaison officer. He will accompany you on your mission. Like you, Major Connor, he speaks the lingo."

Connor exchanged nods with Bradley, but couldn't resist asking the obvious question. "If you're in contact with this Hamid guy, can't he find out the location of Khan?"

"I lost contact with him a week ago," Bradley responded. "But that's not unusual. I left him a coded message about our rendezvous. If he can make it, I'm sure he will."

"When do we go in?" Connor asked.

"In four days, major."

"And tactical support? Can we call in reinforcements? What if we have a man down? Evac by helo may be difficult."

"Almost impossible, I'd say," Colonel Rogers replied. "I'm afraid you'll be on your own. My advice to you is to not get shot."

The initial briefing was wrapped up. Connor went to find Lieutenant Bradley with a question that needed an answer.

"Are you sure you can trust Hamid?"

Bradley shrugged. "As far as you can trust any of them." It was not the response Connor was hoping for. Bradley saw his concern and added, "Hamid comes from a family who have worked the silver mines up there for years. Most mines aren't even marked on our maps, so having someone who can point us to them will save a lot of time. And, anyway, I'm useful to Hamid. It's in his best interests to keep in my good books."

"Explain," said Connor, frowning.

"Hamid's branched out. Silver isn't the only precious thing up there. Years back when the Russians bombed the hell out of the region, they revealed seams of emeralds in the rock. Hamid's family stockpiled munitions left behind when the Russians went home, and ever since they've used the explosives to blast the emeralds out. Their problem, however, was smuggling the gems out and getting a decent price for them."

"And that's where you come in?"

Bradley nodded. "I pay Hamid ten times what he could get from the usual unscrupulous middlemen willing to smuggle them into Pakistan. We're overdue a deal, too. I've got the cash stashed ready. In return he feeds me intel."

"Then we'd better pray nobody's made him a better offer."

CHAPTER THREE
HALO drop

Four days later

The Hercules C-130 climbed to 33,000 feet over the mountains of the Hindu Kush and levelled out. Connor sat alonside his men, still running the mission over in his head. Even after four days there were big gaps in the intel, and no contact from Bradley's man, Hamid. Bradley remained unconcerned, but Connor had to consider the possibility that either something had happened to Hamid or, worse, that his collaboration with US intelligence had been rumbled by the Taliban. If so, Delta Force might be walking into a trap.

Turbulence caused the plane to jolt, rattle and shudder. Lit by a single dim red lamp, everyone sat in silence, the engines droning in their ears. Connor studied Lieutenant Bradley, who was clearly relishing the mission. At least he had something to be grateful for. Rogers could have lumbered him with someone without the necessary combat experience.

The jumpmaster tapped Connor on the shoulder. "Five minutes, major," he shouted through his oxygen mask. "Get ready."

Connor indicated for his team to carry out final checks.

Everything they needed had to be carried: body armour, weapons and ammunition, comms equipment, ration packs, first-aid field kits and sleeping bags, plus the breathing gear they were wearing to survive at this altitude. Together with their parachutes, each man could barely stand under the weight and, despite the cold, they were sweating in their grey-white alpine-style camouflage uniforms.

"One minute!"

The jumpmaster pushed the button to lower the rear cargo door. The howling rush of ice-cold air nearly knocked Connor off his feet. He steadied himself and looked out into the night, hoping to see moonlit, snow-covered peaks, ridges and valleys of the Hindu Kush spread out below. Instead, all he saw was cloud.

"Drop zone ahead! Thirty seconds!"

Connor looked back along the line. Each one of the team gave him a thumbs-up signal in turn, speaking into their throat mics to confirm their checks were complete. In the cockpit the navigator monitored the plane's position closely, waiting for the GPS co-ordinates to match those chosen for the drop. The moment they coincided he flicked a switch and the red light next to the open door changed to green.

"Go... Go... Go..."

Connor hurried down the ramp, launched himself out, and used his arms and legs to control his free fall. Air roared in his ears and rushed

past his face. It was so cold it felt like being in a blast freezer. Suddenly, he broke through the cloud base and saw the ground rushing towards him. He reached for his chute's release cord, but didn't pull it until he was as low as he dared.

The chute snatched Connor from certain death just two hundred metres from impact. He peered down, looking for a decent spot to land. He tugged on the lines to adjust his position. Seconds later his boots sunk into a two-foot drift. Knees bent, he rolled and got a face full of crisp snow.

Dragging in and folding his chute, Connor knew the first task was to find somewhere to bury it. While hastily unclipping his webbing straps he looked around, keen to see where the others landed. Despite the ice and snow casting an eerie paleness in the dark, he could barely make out a thing. "Everyone down OK? Check in, over."

"Sparks here, sir. I'm with Jacko and Sam. We saw you land. We'll be with you in five, over."

"Danny here, sir. I can see Ben. Where are you, over?"

Connor studied his wrist-mounted GPS device and read out his location.

"We'll be with you in ten, sir, over."

Connor waited, listening intently.

Nothing.

"Bradley, do you read me, over?"

Silence.

"Come in, Bradley, over... Listen up, guys, I'm not getting a response from Lieutenant Bradley, so keep your eyes peeled, over."

As his Delta Force team made their way to his position, Connor repeated his calls to Bradley. Grabbing his thermal-imaging binoculars, he scanned the steep valley floor, hoping to detect the lieutenant's heat signature.

"Still nothing?" asked Sparks as he arrived with Jacko and Sam.

Connor shook his head. "Where the hell is he?"

As they waited for Danny and Ben, Connor feared the worst, picturing Bradley unconscious or dead, or maybe crippled on landing. Equally worryingly, Connor knew that a river ran through the valley. He could hear it. It was fast flowing with notorious rapids. Although some parts were covered in thick ice, elsewhere it would be too thin to support a man's weight at this time of year. If Bradley had landed there, he would have punched a hole through it and got swept away. Carrying such heavy kit, he'd stand no chance.

Danny and Ben arrived. Ben was limping heavily. "You OK?" Connor asked.

Ben desperately tried to ignore the shooting

pains. "Yes, sir. Twisted my ankle but I reckon I can walk it off."

"Good." Connor glanced at his watch — zero three fifteen. It was time for him to take some tough decisions. "Sparks, contact CENTCOM and inform them that we've lost Lieutenant Bradley. We'll proceed without him. We have to get to that deserted village and conceal ourselves by dawn. There's simply not enough time to search the whole area. If he's OK and just lost comms then he knows where to head for. If he's in trouble, well, there's not much we can do for him, anyway."

They buried their chutes and set off in single file, Danny taking point duty. Connor said nothing but knew all his team were thinking the same as him. If Bradley was dead or injured, it was only a matter of time before the Taliban found him and they would know ISAF was coming. Connor dismissed the thought as it began to snow — hard.

CHAPTER FOUR
On the trail

They'd landed far up the ninety-six kilometre-
long Panjshir valley, well beyond the wide
expanses of snow-covered fields and leafless
mulberry and walnut groves. Ahead lay a barren,
desolate landscape and the steep trail to the
Khawak Pass, a route across the Hindu Kush
to the fertile northern plains. At over 3,500
metres, Connor was relieved he didn't need to
cross it. Even so, he could tell the air was thin —
breathing was harder, and his backpack felt even
heavier than usual. His team scuffed through
shin-deep snow, which sapped more energy.
The wind had picked up too, and drove the
heavy snowfall into their faces. It felt like being
sandblasted.

They paused as Sparks held a map in front of

Village
meeting
point

Current
location

Landing
site

Connor's face and shone a small torch onto it.

"Sir, despite landing about a kilometre from where we intended, we're making good progress. The abandoned village is half a kilometre further up the valley. We should leave the trail here to get to higher ground. With luck we'll locate the hidden crevice in the rocks and can sit it out until the meeting with Hamid."

At Camp Delta they'd studied recent satellite imagery and old footage taken by drone flights and spotted the crevice on a boulder-strewn ledge overlooking the village. It was ideal. They needed to observe the village before risking entering it. And even if they were sure it was still abandoned, they could only go in during daylight because it was highly likely the Taliban had planted IEDs (improvised explosive devices).

Connor stared into the swirling snow. At least their tracks would be covered now; that was the first piece of good news. He nodded in agreement. "How's Ben doing?" His concern at the way Ben had struggled to keep up was growing.

"Still limping and cursing a lot, sir."

"Can he manage the climb?"

"Guess he'll have to, sir. I'll tell Sam to give him a hand."

Huddled together, Delta Force sat out the rest

of the night in the arrow-shaped crevice about forty-five metres up the mountainside. Although sheltered from the worst of the storm, within minutes of stopping the cold seeped through their uniforms and began to freeze their sweat. Jacko tried out his ultra-thin foil sleeping bag that made him look like a giant roast turkey but soon discarded it, claiming he'd got too hot. Connor repeatedly tried to raise Lieutenant Bradley but all he heard in his earpiece was static hiss.

The snowstorm had stopped, and in the pale light of dawn Connor studied the village below. The nearest buildings were about one hundred and fifty metres away. Using nearby boulders for cover, Jacko and Danny searched the valley with their binoculars for signs of life. Sam blew warm breath into clasped, frozen hands, and then steadied his sniper rifle on a bed of packed snow.

Ben had fallen into a fitful sleep and awoke in agony. His ankle had swollen badly. Connor dosed him up with painkillers and joked about the injury — he could tell Ben was scared of being left behind.

Danny crawled back from the rocks. "Sir, there's nothing moving out there. And the village looks deserted. Want to do a recce?"

The meeting with Hamid had been arranged

by Bradley for 0900 hours. Connor inspected his watch. They had an hour.

"Yes. Sam and Sparks, stay here. Cover us and keep an eye on Ben. Danny and Jacko, you two come with me. Leave your backpacks here. We'll go in light in case we have to move fast."

They descended the steep, narrow path, with Connor leading the way. Initial signs were good. The fresh layer of snow on the main trail lay undisturbed. No one else had passed their way. As they approached the village Connor realised why the place had been abandoned. Walls and buildings lay in ruin. Large, circular depressions in the ground indicated that the village had been shelled — probably years ago, Connor thought — by the Russians. "Jacko, go and check out that first building. And, remember, tread carefully. We'll cover you."

Jacko looked across at a snow-filled ditch. If the Taliban had set booby traps, seeing them under the fresh snow was almost impossible. Every step could be his last. It was what all soldiers feared most. Give them a firefight any day, even incoming RPGs, both were preferable to stepping on an IED that, at best, would blow both legs off. But orders were orders. He gritted his teeth and stepped through.

Jacko entered the roofless house, then emerged after a few seconds. "All clear, sir," he said over the radio. Carefully, he retraced his steps in the snow.

"Good work. The meet with Hamid is in the next building. Just to be safe, we'll use that house as cover and go in around the wall."

They were about to move out when Sparks's voice crackled in Connor's earpiece. He sounded anxious. "Sir, I can see smoke coming from the building just across from you. You're not alone down there."

CHAPTER FIVE
Meeting Hamid

With his back against the wall of the roofless house, Danny gave Connor a leg-up. Connor scanned the neighbouring yard and saw a building in one corner with most of its roof intact. Wisps of wood smoke drifted up through the gaps. The wooden door was closed. Footprints in the snow led from a hole in a building wall on the far side of the yard. Connor reckoned there was more than one set of prints, but he couldn't be sure. Otherwise, most of the area seemed clear. He slipped back down and briefed the others.

"If Bradley got here on his own, he might've arrived during the night — Hamid too," Connor said.

"They might both be in there," Danny suggested.

"Possibly, but we're not taking any chances. Assume it's hostile. Jacko, cover the hole in the building wall. Danny, you're with me. Ready?"

Connor and Danny moved around the broken-down wall, while Jacko sank onto one knee and, M4 firm against his shoulder, got ready for trouble. Connor and Danny darted across the yard, pressing their backs against the wall of the house, either side of the door. Danny nodded and Connor spun and kicked the door in, M4 ready.

Inside, Hamid was sitting cross-legged on the dirt floor, feeding wood onto a small fire. A tin of melted snow hung over the flames and was slowly coming to the boil. Connor's arrival didn't startle him — he'd heard them coming through the snow.

Connor swept the room and saw that the man by the fire was the only person inside. He'd hoped that Bradley would be there too.

The Afghan, wrapped in thick layers to keep warm, had dark hair beneath his turban and jet-black eyes. Connor guessed he was in his mid-forties, but it was hard to tell. "You Hamid?"

Hamid nodded. *"Assalam u alaikum."*

As Connor kept his M4 trained on him, Danny dragged the man to his feet and searched him roughly, just in case explosives or weapons lay beneath his clothes. Hamid did not protest.

"He's clean, sir," Danny announced, letting go. "Just a thick wad of dollars and these." He held out a small drawstring bag filled with uncut gemstones.

Connor clicked on his throat mic. "Sparks, everything all right out there?"

"Yes, major. Can't see a living thing."

Connor relaxed slightly.

"I'm making tea," Hamid explained in Pashto. He gestured towards the fire. Connor nodded and Hamid crouched back down and stared fixedly into the tin of boiling water. "I was expecting Lieutenant Bradley," he added.

"He's been delayed," Connor replied. "So, you know where Mullah Khan is hiding out — and about the meeting ?"

Hamid nodded. "I have some of the information you and Lieutenant Bradley wanted. Khan arrived a month ago with his men. He is in an old silver mine a full day's walk from here. It belonged to my family until Khan came. Now it is his. It is well guarded. I am risking much by telling you this."

"I know, I know. And the meeting?"

"Sorry, I have no idea." Hamid added some tea leaves to the tin. His hand was shaking. "I have risked so much," he repeated.

Hamid glanced up and instantly the major saw the helpless look in the man's eyes. Connor knew something was wrong. The pieces suddenly fell into place: the multiple tracks in the snow; the fact that Hamid had a bag of uncut gems *and* a wad of US dollars. Connor realised Hamid had already met with Bradley! The cash proved it. But Bradley was nowhere to be seen.

Connor's reaction was swift. He knocked Hamid to the floor and kicked the tin of boiling water off its hook to put out the fire. "Code Red!" he shouted into his mic. "It's a trap!"

CHAPTER SIX
Bradley's fate

With the barrel of Danny's light machine gun against Hamid's head, Connor demanded answers. "Where is Lieutenant Bradley? What has happened here?"

"Please," Hamid begged. "I was betrayed. Mullah Khan learned of my meeting with the lieutenant. Khan has my family. He will kill them if I don't do as he asks."

"Where is Bradley?" Connor yelled into the Afghan's face.

"I came yesterday, before it grew dark. Three of Khan's men followed me. Lieutenant Bradley arrived a few hours before dawn. He was exhausted and in great pain. His arm was broken. He didn't explain why he was hurt. He wanted to wait. Said others would come. He must've meant you."

"And?"

Hamid gazed down at the floor. "Khan's men took him outside and killed him."

"Where are Khan's men now?"

Hamid shrugged.

"What about Bradley's body?"

Hamid looked up and went out through the

door and pointed to the mound of snow the opposite side of the yard.

"Show me!" Connor snapped angrily.

"Sir, everything all right, down there, over?"

"Sparks, you and Sam keep us covered. We've got to check something out. Hamid's here and says Khan's men have killed Bradley. There were three of them, maybe more, current whereabouts unknown. Keep your eyes peeled and monitor the airwaves in case they're watching and planning an attack, over."

"Copy that, major. I'm scanning as we speak, over."

Cautiously, they crossed the snow-covered yard. Jacko remained crouched by the wall, continually surveying the rooftops, walls and doorways. Hamid stopped next to a huge snowdrift. "He is in there, major."

Close up, Connor could see drag marks. There was blood too — lots of it. "Did they place an IED? Is it booby-trapped?"

Hamid shook his head.

"Danny, check it out."

Danny climbed up, and looked over the edge of the drift. A rusting metal turret stuck out of the snow, and he quickly realised it must be an old Soviet tank. Carefully, he peered inside the turret. "Oh, Jesus! He's in here, sir." They had bound his hands and cut off his head. Danny reached down and lifted out Bradley's blood-stained helmet. "His radio's broken too. Do you want Jacko and me to get him out?"

"No. Wait." Connor was thinking hard. "Hamid, do Khan's men know about us?"

"I don't think so. I spoke to Bradley in English. The others only spoke Pashto and Dari. I tried to warn Lieutenant Bradley, but by the time he realised, it was too late."

"So, we may still have the element of surprise on our side. Good. Danny, show Hamid our map.

He can point out the location of that silver mine."

Hamid studied the map at length but he was a simple man and struggled with understanding the scale and contour lines. He couldn't point to the mine's location with sufficient certainty to convince Connor. "Right, there's only one alternative," Connor snapped. "You're going to lead us to it, Hamid."

"But they will kill me and my family if they see me with you."

Connor grabbed him sharply by the collar. "That's the least of your problems. Do as you're told and you might just live. But double-cross us and so help me I'll make sure the first bullet in my rifle has your name on it. Jacko, get the others down here. And tell Sparks to inform CENTCOM that we've located Bradley. We'll leave his body where it is. When our mission's complete they can send in another team to extract him."

"Yes, sir," Jacko responded, adding under his breath, "and maybe they'll be coming for our corpses too."

CHAPTER SEVEN
Night strike

Hamid led the way. He said it was best to keep off the main trail. Instead, they followed the path of the river.

"I don't trust Hamid," Sparks snarled.

"Neither do I," Connor responded. "But we've little choice. My biggest worry is whether Khan's men know about us. Hamid said they didn't but we can't be sure."

Danny joined in. "If they knew we were coming wouldn't they have waited and taken us on?"

"Maybe. Or, they decided it was more important to warn Khan that we're onto him."

After a two-hour march, Ben suddenly wilted to his knees and collapsed face down in the snow.

"Ben's exhausted, sir," Jacko declared.

"Just let me rest for five minutes," Ben said, sipping on some water. "I'll be fine."

Connor was uncompromising. "Five minutes, then we move out. Sam, make him eat a couple of chocolate bars to give him a burst of energy."

They carried on up the valley in the direction of the Khawak Pass, with Ben leaning on Jacko for support. An hour before dusk, Hamid led them away from the river to higher ground. They found themselves on a trail overlooking a village.

Connor's eyes narrowed. He could see movement and smoke. Through his binoculars, he observed two Taliban with rifles keeping lookout on the roofs. Several other armed men were wandering about in the central yard. He handed the binoculars to Hamid. "Recognise anyone?"

"Yes. The three men in the yard. They are the ones who killed Lieutenant Bradley."

Connor felt the adrenaline surge and quickly made up his mind. He tied Hamid's hands and sat him down. "Ben, you're staying here with Sam. If Hamid tries to make a run for it, shoot him. The rest of you, come with me."

Under the cover of darkness, Connor led Danny, Jacko and Sparks towards the village. Their night-vision equipment gave the world a strange, eerie glow. Connor and Jacko were armed with silenced M4 carbines, while Danny and Sparks carried FN MK48 light machine guns. Crouching against the wall, close to the courtyard, Connor whispered to Sam over the comms. "We're in position. Update us on current insurgent locations, over."

From the mountainside, Sam peered through the infrared sight of his silenced M110A1 semi-automatic sniper rifle and scanned the village.

"Two still on the roof. Both sitting down, cross-legged. I'll take them out on your command, sir. Just one target in the yard, to your left. Others have gone indoors. Door to building on your right is open and I can see activity inside. The two doors opposite are closed but there is light coming from both houses."

"OK. Confirm line of sight and then on my count, over," Connor replied, signalling Danny and Jacko to move silently to the opposite wall.

Sam lined up the crosshairs of his sight with the first Taliban on the roof. He knew he'd have to take out the second insurgent quickly. "I have the shot, sir, over."

"Three, two, one."

Sam exhaled to relax and squeezed the trigger, absorbing the recoil. The Taliban keeled over. Quickly, he panned his rifle left in a movement he'd practised a dozen times in preparation. Then two rapid shots and the second lookout slumped forward. "Clear, clear, clear... over."

Connor and his team gritted their teeth and rushed into the compound. The lone Taliban standing outside turned in surprise. Jacko fired and the man dropped.

Danny and Sparks kicked open the doors of the houses. The men sitting inside making IEDs were taken completely by surprise.

At the same time, Connor headed towards the open door clutching a grenade. He tossed it inside, spun round against the wall and braced himself for the blast. The building shuddered and dust billowed out through the door and window. He leapt into the doorway and stepped inside. Amid the swirling dust a dozen Taliban lay on the floor. Connor heard a groan. One of them was still alive. Connor saw a bloodied hand reaching for a rifle and he didn't hesitate. A double tap, two shots in rapid succession, and the room was still.

CHAPTER EIGHT
Hamid's village

Connor had just finished securing the area when Sam's voice crackled in his earpiece.

"Sir, there may have been a third lookout. I saw someone running away," he said. "I couldn't get a clear shot, over."

Connor cursed. He knew it was a race against time now. "Sam, bring Ben and Hamid down here. We're moving out. We have to locate that mine and call in the air strike before the alarm is raised, over and out."

Hamid was vague about how long it would take to reach his own village and the silver mines. He kept peering at the struggling Ben, and wondered why on earth they didn't just leave him behind. He thought the Americans foolish. The Taliban, he reckoned, wouldn't hesitate to leave a wounded man behind on such a mission. And he wondered if such ruthlessness lay behind the Taliban's success.

An hour into their march the wind rose to a howl and buffeted their every step. It whipped up the snow and pelted them. Despite Ben abandoning most of his heavy kit, every agonising step took him closer to exhaustion. When he collapsed for the third time, he pleaded for Connor to leave him to rest. "Sir, I'm holding you back. I don't want to be responsible for the failure of our mission. You go on. I'll take my chances."

Connor knew that Ben was right. But he also knew that to leave him there was the equivalent of a death sentence. And he was damned if he was going to lose one of his men. He grabbed Ben's webbing. "Now, you listen to me, Sergeant Saunders. All you have to do is keep placing one foot in front of the other and we'll get there in time. You walk or you die!"

Teeth chattering, Ben reluctantly nodded and tried to get to his feet. Connor helped him up.

Jacko and Sam stepped forward. "We'll carry him, if necessary, sir," said Jacko.

Another five hours wading through the snow, their faces and feet numbed by the cold, they drew close to Hamid's village. The valley had narrowed and the mountains towered over them, shutting out the pale moonlight. The trail was steep and the snow compacted. Connor knew it meant others had recently come their way.

"My house is on the edge of the village," Hamid declared, pointing. "The entrance to the mine is beyond. You cannot see it from the village. It is in a deep ravine."

Connor looked at his team and realised everyone was exhausted. They needed rest and he needed time to figure out how best to proceed. "Where are they holding your family?"

"In a stone hut close to the mine's entrance. I used to keep explosives in it. It has no windows and a strong lock. It makes a good prison."

"Right, then we'll rest at your house. Lead the way."

Hamid swallowed hard but nodded. He knew it was pointless to protest.

Connor took Sparks to one side. "Bury the bulk of our gear here. Just in case."

Entering the enemy's lair, Connor knew that the slightest slip-up and they'd be dead.

CHAPTER NINE
Questions for Hamid

Sergeant Sparks was woken by voices and a baying dog. He blinked. Daylight streamed in through a narrow crack between two grubby blankets being used as curtains. Connor dipped back from the window. "This place is crawling with Taliban."

Connor heard Pashto and Dari being spoken. Barely six feet from the window, three Taliban stood talking and he'd been listening in. They had been there a week and were due to leave tomorrow. "We've got to get a look at that mine," Connor said, thinking aloud.

"I will tell you the way," Hamid replied. "But the guards will recognise me, and there might be trouble. So, you go alone. I will go and see Khan later. I need to free my family."

Connor frowned. There had been something nagging away at him ever since he first met Hamid. If Khan knew Hamid was talking to Bradley, an American, why hadn't Khan ordered his men to kill Hamid as well? Grabbing the Afghan, he posed the question, his tone threatening.

"Yes, it is true Khan feared I would reveal

his presence here," Hamid responded. "That's why Bradley had to die. But my father tried to convince Khan that my only reason for meeting Bradley was to sell our emeralds. Nevertheless, Khan decided to test me. If Bradley gave me money for the emeralds, confirming I spoke the truth, Khan's men were ordered to let me live. I was instructed to return here with both the emeralds and the money, and give both to Khan. Only then will he release my family."

Connor scratched his beard thoughtfully. It sort of made sense.

Filled with painkillers, Ben slept soundly. Hamid boiled some water and Sam added it to their powdered ration packs. As they ate, a plan began to form in Connor's head. "Hamid, go and fetch all your spare clothes. If we're going to have any chance of getting to the mine in daylight we need to be disguised."

Hamid disappeared into another room. Danny followed him.

"Sam, you stay here with Ben, and keep a close eye on Hamid. We'll do a recce, and with any luck get the co-ordinates of the mine. We'll radio them back to CENTCOM and get the hell out of here as soon as it's dark."

Jacko was busy cleaning his rifle. "So you

believe our little friend's story, do you, sir?"

Connor shrugged. "Right now, I don't think we have much choice."

Jacko pulled a face. "If you ask me, his story doesn't entirely add up. Why was he still there when we arrived at that abandoned village? Why didn't he leave with Khan's men? After all, he had the cash and emeralds."

There was no denying it, Jacko had a point. Connor couldn't think of a reason why Hamid had stayed on at the village either. When the Afghan returned clutching a pile of unwashed clothes, Jacko fired the question at him. Hamid put the clothes down. "I told Khan's men I was feeling ill and needed to rest a while. Bradley had said there were others coming. I stayed on to warn you."

It was the perfect answer. Too perfect? Connor wondered.

CHAPTER TEN
Double crossed?

Connor, Sparks, Danny and Jacko left Hamid's house wearing clothes the Afghan had given them. They walked slowly through the village. The place was a hive of activity, with small gatherings of Taliban squatting about fires and talking of war. There were so many, few gave Connor and his men more than a second glance. Connor noticed several cages full of chickens and half a dozen tethered goats. He suspected that a feast was going to be prepared. Maybe, just maybe, they'd timed their visit perfectly.

Following Hamid's instructions they continued along a path that climbed northwards, away from the village. With the storm having passed and the sun now out, Connor was struck by the barren, almost brutal, landscape of snow and rock. He figured that if it wasn't for the silver and emeralds, few would even try to eke out an existence in such a remote and unforgiving place.

The path quickly levelled out. Either side, sheer rock faces rose high into the sky. To their left, the ground fell away steeply to form a deep ravine. At the end was the entrance to the mine, a small stone building, and six Taliban guards.

Danny appeared at Connor's shoulder. "Reminds me of the caves at Tora Bora," he whispered. "So well concealed that air strikes won't work."

Connor nodded. Reaching to his wrist, he felt for his GPS device hidden beneath his sleeve and pressed the button that would record his precise position. He now had the information Rogers needed to target the air strike but knew that it was doomed to failure. Sparks read his thoughts. "Sir, it would be better if we could blow the entrance ourselves. But we haven't got the ordnance to do that."

Connor remembered how Bradley had told him that Hamid's family had stockpiled old Russian munitions. "No, but I know a man who has."

A sudden commotion behind them made Connor and his men turn sharply. They could only look on in horror. Hamid was waving an AK-47 rifle triumphantly in the air. Behind him, Taliban were dragging Sam and Ben. And behind them came twenty more Taliban, all shouting and cheering and waving their rifles, all baying for the blood of the American infidels to be spilled.

"Why, the dirty, double-crossing little rat," Jacko snarled.

Sensing Jacko was reaching for his concealed handgun, Connor grabbed his arm. "Wait. It might not be quite what it seems." Connor had noticed that Hamid had not pointed them out and figured there had to be a reason why. "I reckon someone came to his house and saw Ben and Sam. Hamid had no choice but to make out he'd captured them on his return journey."

"Khan will never buy it," Danny replied.

"No, maybe not, but it has bought both Hamid and us some time." Connor came to a snap decision. "He's not going to give us away. At least, not yet. Come on, we'll join the crowd. They're heading inside the mine."

Merging with the throng, Connor and his men entered the silver mine. The entrance, little bigger than a doorway, led to a tunnel directly into the mountainside. Well lit by lamps, Connor noted several narrow side shafts piled high with weapons and boxes of ammunition. The crowd continued on, the ear-splitting cacophony of shouting echoing and reverberating. Deep into the mine, the tunnel opened up into a ninety foot cavern. Water dripped from the ceiling and the uneven floor was wet and slippery underfoot. There were tables and chairs and filthy old mattresses, some covered in richly embroidered blankets. On a raised platform sat a plump man, wearing a black turban. He had a large scar on his face. "So we meet at last, Mullah Khan," Connor muttered hatefully under his breath.

Sam and Ben were thrown onto the floor at Khan's feet. The crowd fell silent. Hamid stepped forward. "These infidels came with Lieutenant Bradley. I have tricked them. They are a gift to you, Mullah Khan."

A tall Taliban fighter standing at Khan's shoulder leaned forward and whispered to him. Khan then spoke. "These men attacked a village. Many of our brothers perished. Rafiq, here, was there. He says there were other infidels."

"Yes, but they were killed," Hamid lied. "I have come to ask you to release my family. I have done what you asked."

"How do I know you speak the truth? The men I sent with you to meet Lieutenant Bradley are dead too."

Fumbling beneath his shirt, Hamid produced his drawstring bag of emeralds and wad of American dollars. "For you, sir. And the Taliban cause. They will buy many weapons."

Khan thought long and hard before announcing his decision. "Very well, I shall release your family." He then addressed the crowd. "Brothers, this is our last evening together. Tonight, we shall have a great feast here, *inshallah*. Tomorrow you leave. And you all know your missions. A week from now the streets of Kabul shall run with the blood of the infidel."

Cries of *Allahu Akbar* rang out.

"And tonight we shall film these two infidels pleading for mercy. Then, at midnight, you, Hamid, will have the honour of cutting off their heads."

Standing at the back of the crowd, Connor whispered, "I've heard enough. Come on, we've got work to do."

Having watched Sam and Ben being locked up in the heavily guarded stone hut close to the mine's entrance, Connor and the rest of his team retraced their steps to Hamid's house and set about figuring out a rescue plan.

A worried Hamid returned half an hour later with his father, wife and two children. They looked hungry and scared out of their wits, their fear doubling on seeing Connor and his men. Hamid paced the room anxiously. "I cannot do it. Allah forbids it. I will not cut off their heads. We must run away. Otherwise Khan will kill us too."

"If all goes well you won't need to," Connor replied. He took hold of the Afghan and sat him down. "Now, listen, are there any other entrances to that mine?"

Hamid shook his head.

"Good. Where do you keep those old Russian explosives you use to blast out the emeralds?"

Hamid looked up. "In an outbuilding. Why?"

"Jacko, go with him and fetch as much as you can carry. Sparks, relay the GPS co-ordinates of the mine and village to CENTCOM and inform them the meeting is being held tonight. Also, make it clear that an air strike will only have limited success on the mine and so we're going to try and destroy it ourselves. To give us time to get clear, set Zero Hour for the F-16s at 2300 hours. Arrange an evac by helo for us one kilometre back along the trail, timed to coincide."

Connor's plan was simple, to wait until the feast inside the mine was under way and then blast the mine tunnel with enough plastic explosive to cause it to collapse. Even if some of the Taliban survived the explosion, they'd be entombed. But there were complications.

"We can't lay an old-fashioned wire or Bickford fuse," Danny noted, scratching his beard thoughtfully. "There are too many guards. They'd see it. And, we haven't any remote detonators, sir."

Connor already had the problem covered. "That's not quite true, Danny. We'll improvise. Go and fetch the Switchblade that Sam was carrying in his backpack."

"Yes, sir." Danny grinned. He realised what Connor had in mind. Switchblade was the latest high-tech mini-drone, so new that it had barely finished official testing.

Jacko and Hamid returned lugging two large sacks filled with plastic explosive. Connor inspected them. "Excellent. There's enough there to demolish half a mountain. Now, Hamid, we need three wooden crates and a pile of cooking vessels. And ask your wife to boil up a large pot of vegetables."

"Vegetables?" Hamid frowned in bewilderment but did as asked.

As dusk fell and the Taliban began making their way to the feast, Delta Force prepared the wooden crates. In one, they placed pots of steaming vegetables. The other two were crammed with explosives. Hamid's wife draped cloths over all three. They were ready. Connor ran through everyone's role one last time. Hamid appeared extremely nervous, and he had good reason to be.

CHAPTER ELEVEN
Connor's plan

Positioning themselves overlooking the ravine, Connor and Sparks watched through their night-vision binoculars as the last of the visiting Taliban fighters entered the mine. It was 2200. The nearby stone hut remained under guard. Connor was relieved, as it meant that Ben and Sam were inside, and hadn't yet been taken to Khan.

Putting down his bins, Connor opened the Switchblade pack. First, he removed the metre-long cylindrical launcher. The electric-powered mini-drone was inside. He set it up on a flattish piece of ground. Then he peered into the shoebox-shaped viewer which would display the real-time video feed from a tiny camera on the drone's nose.

Sparks kept watch. "They're on their way," he said after a long wait, pointing. "Game on."

Hamid walked one pace ahead of Danny and Jacko towards the entrance to the mine. Each carried a crate. Hamid was shaking but hoped the darkness would conceal his terror. He stopped abruptly when challenged by a Taliban sentry. "I bring extra food at the request of Mullah Khan.

There is much feasting to be done."

The sentry stepped forward and lifted the cloth. Steam from the pot of vegetables filled the air. Replacing the cloth, he nodded and stepped back, gesturing with his rifle towards the lamplight spilling from the entrance. Barely able to hold the crate steady, Hamid thanked him and entered the mine, the heavily disguised Danny and Jacko following quickly on his heels, unchallenged.

"So far so good." Stage one of Connor's plan was complete. He grabbed hold of the small hand-held panel of switches and joystick he'd use to control the mini-drone once it was launched. But first he had to wait for the others to place the charges and make it out of the mine safely.

Hamid, Jacko and Danny moved in single file through the tunnel. Connor had instructed them to place the crates on the left-hand side, sixty paces from the entrance. As they counted, they heard Mullah Khan leading his men in prayer. The voices boomed and echoed.

"Here," Danny declared. He put down his crate. Jacko placed his on top, and Hamid's topped the stack. Danny could see rows of Taliban kneeling on prayer cushions in the main cavern, their backs to him, all facing Khan sitting cross-legged on his raised platform. He thought of Bradley and of sweet revenge.

Turning to leave they were confronted by Khan's right-hand man, Rafiq. He gazed at them with suspicion. "What are you doing? Why aren't you praying?"

"I have brought extra food," Hamid explained. His feeble voice betrayed his fear.

"I see." Rafiq frowned. "Now you have brought it, you can go and pray."

"No, I must..." Hamid pleaded. "I must go home."

"Nonsense. Mullah Khan has bestowed the greatest honour on you. By your sword hand the infidels shall die. But, come, first you must pray."

"That's why I must go home," Hamid continued. "I wish to use my father's sword. It has the finest blade. Allah demands a clean cut."

"You can use my sword," Rafiq snapped, seizing Hamid's arm.

2220. Connor gazed anxiously at the entrance to the mine. "Damn it, what's keeping them? They should have come out by now."

CHAPTER TWELVE
Neat flying

Jacko's strike to Rafiq's throat made the Taliban's eyes bulge. A second later he was dead, his neck snapped by a sharp twist. "Let's get the hell out of here," Jacko snarled, dragging the body into one of the side tunnels.

The second they emerged from the mine, Sparks headed off to join them. Connor launched the Switchblade mini-drone from its carrier. It barely made a sound as it climbed into the night sky. Connor peered into the video viewfinder and used the joystick to gain control. He sent it on a wide arc, allowing it to gather speed, and then set a course into the ravine and the mine's entrance.

Once beyond sight of the guards, Sparks distributed weapons to Danny and Jacko, who were keen to strip off their disguises.

Hamid's work was done. "Go," Sparks said to him. "And take your family as far away from here as you can get."

Connor's palms were all sweaty and his pulse raced. The live feed from the drone's tiny nose-mounted camera took a little getting used to, and he had only one shot at getting it right. Fail and the mission would be a disaster. Concentrating hard, he applied gentle pressure on the joystick to correct the drone's path. Travelling at forty kilometres an hour, it flew directly towards the entrance. Connor flicked a switch to arm the small two-pound explosive warhead. Suddenly the drone was inside the tunnel. Connor saw flashes as it flew past each lamp lining the walls. "Where are they? Where are they?" he muttered. Then he saw the crates and aimed the drone right at them.

The screen in Connor's viewfinder went blank.

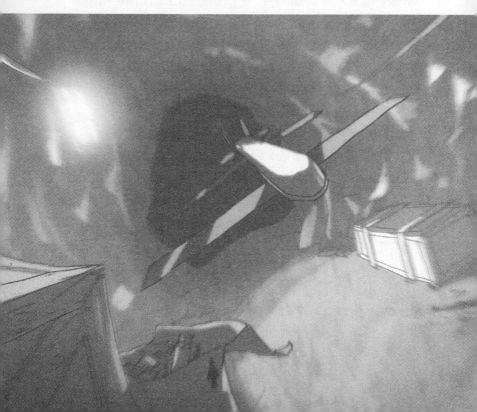

A flash emerged from the mine's entrance. Then a loud rumble and the earth shook. Finally debris, dust and smoke blasted out. Leaping up, Connor ran.

Dazed, the guards outside staggered about in shock. Jacko, Danny and Sparks let rip with their carbines and lightweight machine guns as they ran down into the ravine. In seconds the guards were dead. Jacko shot through the lock on the stone hut, swung the door open and helped Ben and Sam out.

Shouldering Ben, they headed out of the ravine to where Connor was waiting. "We've got just twenty minutes to make our evac rendezvous, and it's a kilometre from here. We're going to have to run. Ben, can you make it?"

"I can try, sir."

Connor saw that Ben still couldn't put his weight on his injured ankle. "No. We'll take it in turns carrying you. Danny and Sparks, take the first hundred metres."

Barely midway through the village they could hear the approaching F-16s. Desperately, Sparks tried to raise CENTCOM and get them to delay the strike. He looked to the heavens and cursed. "Too late, sir, they've been given the green light. They'll be here any second."

Heaving for breath, they ran on, Ben slung between Connor's and Danny's shoulders. They made it just past Hamid's house when the F-16s roared overhead and their bombs slammed into the village. The whole area erupted. Balls of fire engulfed the valley. The blasts flung Connor and his team through the air. Landing heavily in deep drifts of snow they felt the searing heat as debris rained down on them.

Winded, Connor rolled over. Jacko was sat up, coughing. Danny and Sam complained they'd gone temporarily deaf. Realising everyone was alive, Ben let out a primal scream and smacked his fists into the snow.

Slowly, they dragged themselves to their feet. "Sir," Sparks called out, his face blackened with soot. "Made contact with our helo. She's landed. They know we're slightly behind schedule and will wait for us."

"How very generous of them," Connor muttered. He managed to stagger a few paces before stopping to catch his breath. "Guys, the next time I get a text from Colonel Rogers, remind me to ignore it!"

WEAPONS and GEAR

M4 CARBINE (5.56MM)
with Delta Force accessories

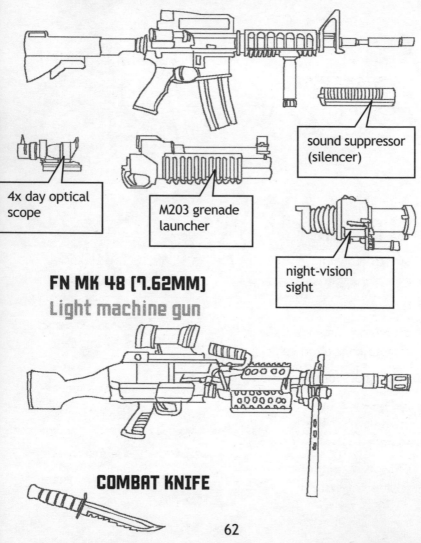

sound suppressor (silencer)

4x day optical scope

M203 grenade launcher

night-vision sight

FN MK 48 (7.62MM)
Light machine gun

COMBAT KNIFE

M110A1 [7.62MM]
Semi-automatic sniper system

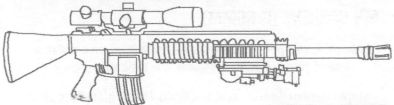

GLOCK 17 [9MM]

NIGHT-VISION SCOPE

GLOSSARY

air strike bombs dropped by a plane onto a target

bins binoculars

drone an unmanned remote-controlled vehicle

evac short for evacuation

fedayeen someone who gives up their life for something they believe

GPS short for global positioning system

IEDs Improvised Explosive Devices, home-made bombs triggered by remote control

infidels refers to someone without faith, in this case, a non-Muslim

intel short for intelligence

ISAF International Security Assistance Force – the NATO-led mission in Afghanistan

rendezvous a pre-arranged meeting

NEXT mission!

KILL OR CAPTURE

In Book 4, 347 prisoners escape from a jail in Kandahar. One of them is Jabir Hassani — a Taliban warlord.

Major Nathan Connor and his Delta Force team must kill or capture Hassani, and put a stop to his plans.

Mid-morning, Major Nathan Connor and his team arrived in their modified GMV at the outskirts of Kandahar's old town. It was chaos. Dozens of armoured vehicles were parked up close together. Groups of ANA soldiers stood around at road junctions, while others pulled razor wire across the road to form a barricade. Black Hawk helicopters roared overhead, circling at low altitude. In the searing heat, dozens of US marines in body armour and full kit were standing around clutching their weapons, sweating and waiting nervously to move out; others were running to and fro as final preparations were made. General Patterson's parting orders rang in Connor's ears — find Jabir and this time I don't give a damn whether you kill or capture him!

Continued in: Task Force Delta — Kill or Capture